HELLO, I'm THEA!

I'm *Geronimo Stilton*'s sister. As I'm sure you know from my brother's bestselling novels, I'm a special correspondent for *The Rodent's Gazette*, Mouse Island's most famouse newspaper. Unlike my 'fraidy mouse brother, I absolutely adore traveling, having adventures, and meeting rodents from all around the world!

The adventure I want to tell you about begins at Mouseford Academy, the school I went to when I was a young mouseling. I had such a great experience there as a student that I came back to teach a journalism class.

When I returned as a grown mouse, I met five really special students: Colette, Nicky, Pamela, Paulina, and Violet. You could hardly imagine five more different mouselings, but they became great friends right away. And they liked me so much that they decided to name their group after me: the Thea Sisters! I was so touched by that, I decided to write about their adventures. So turn the page to read a fabumouse adventure about the

THEA SISTERS!

Name: Nicky

Nickname: Nic

Home: Australia

Secret ambition: Wants to be an ecologist.

Loves: Open spaces and nature.

Strengths: She is always in a good mood, as long as she's outdoors!

Weaknesses: She can't sit still!

Secret: Nicky is claustrophobic—she can't stand being in small, tight places.

Nicky

Nicky

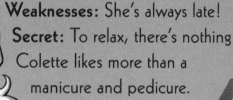

COLETTE

Name: Colette

Nickname: It's Colette, please. (She can't stand nicknames.)

Home: France

Secret ambition: Colette is very particular about her appearance. She wants to be a fashion writer.

Loves: The color pink.

Strengths: She's energetic and full of great ideas.

Weaknesses: She's always late!

Secret: To relax, there's nothing Colette likes more than a manicure and pedicure.

Colette

Name: Violet
Nickname: Vi
Home: China
Secret ambition: Wants to become a great violinist.
Loves: Books! She is a real intellectual, just like my brother, Geronimo.
Strengths: She's detail-oriented and always open to new things.
Weaknesses: She is a bit sensitive and can't stand being teased. And if she doesn't get enough sleep, she can be a real grouch!
Secret: She likes to unwind by listening to classical music and drinking green tea.

VIOLET

Violet

Name: Paulina
Nickname: Polly
Home: Peru
Secret ambition: Wants to be a scientist.
Loves: Traveling and meeting people from all over the world. She is also very close to her sister, Maria.
Strengths: Loves helping other rodents.
Weaknesses: She's shy and can be a bit clumsy.
Secret: She is a computer genius!

PAULINA

PAULINA

Name: Pamela
Nickname: Pam
Home: Tanzania

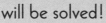
PAMELA

Secret ambition: Wants to become a sports journalist or a car mechanic.

Loves: Pizza, pizza, and more pizza! She'd eat pizza for breakfast if she could.

Strengths: She is a peacemaker. She can't stand arguments.

Weaknesses: She is very impulsive.

Secret: Give her a screwdriver and any mechanical problem will be solved!

Pamela

Geronimo Stilton

Thea Stilton
AND THE SECRET
OF THE OLD CASTLE

Scholastic Inc.

New York   Toronto   London   Auckland
Sydney   Mexico City   New Delhi   Hong Kong

ISBN 978-0-545-34107-3

Published by Scholastic Inc., 557 Broadway, New York, NY 10012. SCHOLASTIC and associated logos are trademarks and/or registered trademarks of Scholastic Inc.

Text by Thea Stilton
Original title *Il segreto del castello scozzese*
Cover by Arianna Rea, Paolo Ferrante, and Ketty Formaggio
Illustrations by Jacopo Brandi, Alessandro Battan, Elisa Falcone, Claudia Forcelloni, Daniela Geremia, Rosa La Barbera, Roberta Pierpaoli, Arianna Rea, Maurizio Roggerone, and Roberta Tedeschi
Color by Alessandra Bracaglia, Ketty Formaggio, Elena Sanjust, and Micaela Tangorra
Graphics by Paola Cantoni

Special thanks to Beth Dunfey
Translated by Emily Clement
Interior design by Kay Petronio

12 11 10 9 8 7 6 5 4 3 2   12 13 14 15 16 17/0

Printed in the U.S.A.   40
First printing, March 2012

A MOTORCYCLE MOUSE!

It was a beautiful May evening in New Mouse City. I had just returned from a fabumouse trip across Mouse Island on my **motorcycle**, and I was in a great mood.

Oh, pardon me. I almost forgot to introduce myself! My name is Thea Stilton, and I am a special correspondent for *The Rodent's Gazette*, the newspaper run by my brother, Geronimo. I **travel** a lot for work, and my motorcycle is always by my side, like a true FRIEND!

That evening, I had just parked outside my apartment when my cell phone **beeped**.

BEE-BEE-BEEP! BEE-BEE-BEEP!

I had a text message. It was a picture of my good friends *Colette*, *Nicky*, PAMELA, PAULINA, and **Violet**, seated on three **brand-new** motorcycles!

I called them right away. "Thundering cattails, you look fantastic on those motorcycles, mouselets!"

Paulina laughed. "Thanks, Thea! I thought you'd approve. We're in Scotland, on a **mission** in the Highlands!"

"Traveling by motorcycle is great," Pamela added. "It's almost like flying!"

That was the *enthusiasm* that had first drawn me to the Thea Sisters. Ever since I'd taught them in a journalism class at **MOUSEFORD ACADEMY**, these five incredible mouselets had never ceased to amaze me. They were my best students!

Seeing them travel by motorcycle made me feel as though I were right there with them.

Of course, I was wondering what they were up to in Scotland. And I'll bet you are, too! So get ready for a **RIP-ROARING** new adventure with the Thea Sisters!

SCOTLAND

INVERNESS

HIGHLANDS

EDINBURGH

LOWLANDS

Capital: Edinburgh
Surface area: 30,414 square miles
Population: 5,222,100 inhabitants, although the population is not evenly distributed. In the industrial city of Glasgow, there are around 8,700 people per square mile, while in some parts of the Highlands, there are only 23!

Scotland is one of the four nations that make up the **United Kingdom**, along with England, Wales, and Northern Ireland. It occupies the northern part of the island of Great Britain. Although it is part of the United Kingdom, Scotland has its own legal system and its own parliament. It was once an independent region known by the name **Caledonia**.

THE HIGHLANDS

Scotland is traditionally divided into the *Highlands* and the *Lowlands*. This division isn't just geographic: The Highlands are different from the Lowlands in language and traditions. The culture in the Highlands is similar to Irish culture. The Irish and the Highlanders share a language — Gaelic — and a traditional style of Celtic music.

The Highlands are dominated by large and impressive mountain ranges and are sparsely populated. Inverness is considered the administrative center of the Scottish Highlands.

● THE ISLE OF SKYE

The **Isle of Skye** is the largest of the Inner Hebrides islands (that is, the set of islands closest to the mainland). Its coastline is rugged, and the countryside is wild and breathtaking.

BRiDGET MACNAMOUSE

The Scottish saga began on a day like any other at **MOUSEFORD ACADEMY**.

During a break between classes, Violet ran into her friend and fellow student **Bridget MacNamouse**. Bridget was a **shy** and quiet mouselet. She was always kind to everyone, but she wasn't very talkative.

Nonetheless, Bridget and Violet had become good friends. They shared the same deep **Love** of music. Bridget was Scottish, and the two mouselets had started to tell each other stories about the culture and traditions of their countries.

Violet was on her way to class when she spotted Bridget. She was struck by the

worried **LOOK** on Bridget's snout, so she scurried over to squeak with her. "Is everything okay, Bridget? We're still meeting in the auditorium to practice our duets this afternoon, right?"

Bridget **SMILED**, but she looked as stressed as a rat in a maze. "I can't, Violet. I have to

Bridget
MacNamouse

CLANS

Clan is a word that comes from Gaelic, the ancient language of the Celts. In Gaelic, *clann* means "children" or "family." A clan is a group of people descended from a common ancestor or forefather.

leave for Scotland at once! There's a clan reunion to decide what's going to happen to the **MacNamouse** family castle, and I can't miss it!"

Violet was curious. "Is this the ancient **family** castle you've told me so much about?"

"That's it!" Bridget said. "It's in **terrible** shape, and we heirs need to decide what to do immediately. That's why I have to **LEAVE** today."

"I'm sure everything will work out. Plus,

you'll get to see your family!" Violet tried to **REASSURE** Bridget.

Bridget sighed heavily. "That's true, but unfortunately, I don't think it's going to be a fun family party. My uncles and cousins do nothing but **BICKER**! But I *have* to be there: I have a **MISSION** to complete! My grandfather loved that castle."

CLUE!

Violet squeezed Bridget's paws **tightly**. "As soon as you get home, contact me, okay? Keep me posted on everything that's going on."

Just then, Nicky popped out of the math classroom. "**Violet!!!** Come on, move those paws! Class is about to start!"

Bridget and Violet said a quick good-bye, and Violet scampered to class.

 What did Bridget mean when she said she had a "mission to complete"?

A CASTLE TO SAVE!

The next evening, Violet kept checking her **e-mail**. She was hoping to find a note from Bridget, but there weren't any new messages.

She was about to try calling her **friend** on her cell phone when a text message arrived from **Bridget**.

MacNamouse
Castle is in
danger. I need
your help!
Bridget

MacNamouse Castle in **DANGER**?! What could have happened?!

Violet immediately dialed Bridget, but all she heard on the other end was buzzing. She tried again, with the same result.

So Violet **RAN** to Paulina's room. Nicky, Pamela, and

Colette were there, too, doing homework.

Violet showed them Bridget's message. "See?! Bridget's asking for **HELP**! She was so worried yesterday. She was talking about some kind of **mission**."

"She didn't call you to explain? She just sent you a text message?" Colette asked.

"Yes, and when I tried calling her back, I just got this weird buzzing sound!" Violet replied. "So what are we going to do? We can't ignore her cry for help!"

The friends exchanged serious **LOOKS**.

Pam squeaked first. "Sizzling spark plugs, you're right, Violet! Bridget needs us!"

"I'm with Pam!" Nicky added.

As always, Paulina was **practical**. "First we need to **LEARN** a little more about this castle."

"**GREAT IDEA!**" Violet exclaimed.

"I think I know someone who can help."

Paulina's EXCITEMENT quickly faded. "Oh, nooo! Don't tell me you're thinking of PROFESSOR RATTCLIFF!"

"Of course!" Violet confirmed. "She knows Bridget really well. She's Scottish, too, and I see them chattering all the time."

Colette nodded. "And she's studied the tRADITIONS of Scotland. Once, she helped me with some research on Scottish kilts and tartans*!"

"Fine, let's go to the professor," Pam mumbled, "even though she isn't exactly warm and furry. . . ."

Margaret Rattcliff, professor of literature and creative writing, was in her office. Of all the teachers at the academy, she was the STRICTEST. She kept her students on their PAWS. There wasn't a more

---

* Do you want to know more about Scottish *kilts* and *tartans*? Turn to page 14!

feared professor at **MOUSEFORD**!

Violet showed her Bridget's message right away. "I'm very worried about Bridget MacNamouse, Professor. See? She's asking for help!"

When the professor read Bridget's message, her expression changed **IMMEDIATELY**. "Do you have any idea what this means?"

"Not yet," Violet admitted. "But Bridget was very UPSET before she left!"

The **PROFESSOR** nodded. "This castle is one of the oldest in all of Scotland. It's on the Isle of Skye, and it's a real treasure! Unfortunately, most of Alistair MacNamouse's

Professor Margaret Rattcliff

THE KILT

A **kilt** is a pleated knee-length garment similar to a skirt. It's usually made of **tartan**. Tartan is a material made of wool with a particular plaid design woven into it using many different colors.

In Scotland, every clan has its own motto and its own distinctive tartan pattern. For those who don't have their own tartans, there are free patterns. Anyone can create a personalized tartan and register it with the **Scottish Register of Tartans**.

The kilt as we know it today originated in the Scottish Highlands in the sixteenth century. In earlier centuries, there was the *feileadh mor* (or "big kilt"), a simple cloth about five yards long, which was wrapped around the waist and held in place by a belt. The *feileadh mor* was eventually simplified to be just a belt and a shorter skirt. This new model was given the name *feileadh beg,* or "little kilt."

The kilt is usually worn with a **sporran** (in Gaelic, this means "pocket" or "purse") — that is, a leather pouch. The sporran holds personal items, since the kilt doesn't have pockets.

descendants have never attained the **STATUS** of their esteemed ancestor."

Nicky looked puzzled.

"She means that Bridget's great-great-great-grandfather was an **honorable** mouse, but most of her relatives are **SLIMY** sewer rats," Paulina whispered. Professor Rattcliff often squeaked in this old-fashioned way, and Paulina was an expert at interpreting!

Professor Rattcliff sprang up, rummaged through her **bookshelves**, and pulled out two fat volumes and one thinner one.

"The History of Scotland, Scottish Castles and Legends, and *A Guide to the Isle of Skye*!" she said, giving the books to Pamela. "You must prepare if you want to go to Scotland."

"**GO TO SCOTLAND?!?**" the mouselets all exclaimed.

"Indeed!" said the professor, as if it were obvious. "Someone must investigate what's happening UP thERE! And it seems Bridget has put her FAITH in you."

Professor Rattcliff stepped back and looked each of the mouselets over from snout to paw. Then she nodded. "I have faith in you, too! Come! Let's go see the headmaster."

GLOBE-TROTTERS

Headmaster *Octavius de Mousus* wasn't quite as sure that the mouselets should jet off to Scotland. But Professor Rattcliff convinced him to make several phone calls. He moved **SEAS** and **MOUNTAINS** in an attempt to get in touch with Bridget. But it was no use. She seemed to have disappeared!

After much discussion with Professor Rattcliff, the headmaster finally gave the Thea Sisters permission to head to the **Isle of Skye**.

"But I can only give you four days, including the weekend!" the headmaster warned them.

The Thea Sisters packed their bags **quicker** than you can say "chewy cheesecake with chocolate on top." Even

Colette managed to fit everything into a single backpack (although it was an *enormouse* backpack, complete with **wheels**!).

The next morning, they boarded **Vince Guymouse's** hydroplane bright and early. They reached Mouse Island just in time to catch the first available **FLiGHT** to Glasgow.

THE CITIES OF SCOTLAND

- Edinburgh, the capital of Scotland, is located on the east coast and is known as the Athens of the North, because of its historic beauty. Edinburgh's Old Town gives visitors the flavor of ancient Scotland.

- Glasgow may not be as pretty as Edinburgh, but it has many other things to recommend it. It is the economic capital of Scotland and also has the largest population.

- Aberdeen is Scotland's most important port city, because oil tankers from the North Sea dock there.

Violet sent a text message—the last of many—to Bridget to let her know when they'd arrive.

But why wasn't Bridget responding?!

The mouselets settled in for a long flight. Violet and Paulina pulled out the BOOKS

Professor Rattcliff had loaned them. Unfortunately, the guide to the Isle of Skye was **old**, and the information about how to get there was no longer reliable.

Meanwhile, Pamela, Nicky, and Colette were making friends with two ratlings from Spain who had planned a **trip** to Scotland. They had up-to-date road maps. By the time the five mice **LANDED**, Pamela knew everything there was to know about the Scottish highway system!

EVERYONE HOP ON!

"Let's rent motorcycles!" Pamela exclaimed as soon as they left the airport.

"*Motorcycles!*" Violet replied. "Are you kidding?"

"No, I'm **SERIOUS**," Pam replied. "It's almost two hundred miles to the Skye Bridge in Kyle of Lochalsh. On a bike, we can get there in less than four and a half hours!"

Violet wasn't convinced. "I was thinking we could get there by TRAIN."

"Yes, but how would we get around the island?" Pam said. "We need a way to get to the castle. We could rent a car, of course, but the roads are so narrow and winding that it'll be hard to maneuver. With motorcycles, it'll be much easier to get around!"

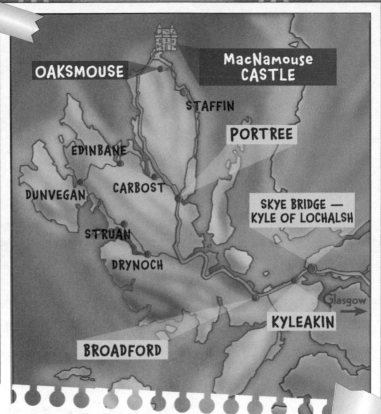

OAKSMOUSE

MacNamouse CASTLE

STAFFIN

PORTREE

EDINBANE

DUNVEGAN

CARBOST

SKYE BRIDGE —
KYLE OF LOCHALSH

STRUAN

DRYNOCH

Glasgow →

KYLEAKIN

BROADFORD

THE MOUSELETS' ROAD TRIP!

To get to the Isle of Skye, the Thea Sisters must reach the town **Kyle of Lochalsh**. From there, they can cross a bridge to the island. Then they'll have to head farther north. **MacNamouse Castle** stands close to the village of **Oaksmouse**, right on the northern coast of the island.

"Yes, but we'll still need to cross the island—it's fifty miles!" Colette said **anxiously**, fluffing her fur. "That's going to do some serious damage to my 'do!"

But Pam wasn't giving up easily. "Colette, the whole drive is along the coast. Think of all those **breathtaking** landscapes!"

"I vote for the motorcycles!" Nicky exclaimed, raising her paw **ENTHUSIASTICALLY**. "We're going to the Highlands, mouselets. Don't you want to enjoy the countryside?!"

Paulina nodded. **"GOOD POINT, NICKY!"**

"Well, okay, I guess we can try it," Violet said, giving in.

Only Colette was still uncertain. "What am I going to do with my backpack?"

"Don't **worry**, Colette," Pamela replied. "We'll rent motorcycles with **BIG** storage

compartments. You'll see—it'll be like a wardrobe on wheels!"

Colette responded with a nervous SMILE.

Just outside the airport, the mouselets found a place to rent everything they needed: three motorcycles in perfect shape, filled with gasoline; five helmets in different COLORS; jackets that were light but made of a weather-resistant fabric; up-to-date road maps; and an emergency kit in case of a breakdown.

helmet

jacket

up-to-date maps

emergency kit

They had just left Glasgow when a fine **rain** started to fall.

"**Brr**!" said Paulina, **shivering**.

"That's just how it is on the British Isles," said Colette, shrugging. "It's frightful for the fur, but what can you do?"

They continued driving. After an hour's journey, they spotted Loch Lomond, the largest **lake** in Great Britain. A patch of blue sky appeared, and the sun peeked through the clouds. It **lit up** the rippling surface of the lake. On the other side, green hills SPARKLED in the mist.

"Look at all the sheep!" Nicky squealed with excitement, pointing to a white patch that was moving slowly on one of the hills. She was from a sheep farm in Australia, so for her, seeing those sheep felt like coming home.

Suddenly, they spotted the top of a hill completely covered with a blanket of purplish heather in bloom.

"How gorgeous!" Colette exclaimed with a sigh.

THE LOCHS

Lakes in Scotland are called lochs and can be filled with freshwater or salt water. Lakes filled with salt water are connected to the sea and can reach inland for many miles. Their shape is always long and narrow. Many of these lakes are connected artificially so they can be used as waterways. The Caledonian Canal, for example, is a canal that connects Loch Lochy, Loch Oich, Loch Ness, and Loch Linnhe.

A SPECTACULAR SIGHT!

The mouselets zoomed along, stopping every now and then to admire the **beautiful** countryside. The mountaintops were already sprinkled with **snow**. The sight of dazzling sunshine reflected by Loch Linnhe forced the Thea Sisters to stop: It was **AMAZING!**

The mouselets **stretched** their paws. A check of the map showed they still had forty-six more miles before they reached Kyle of Lochalsh, and they were starting to feel a little **tired**. It had been a long journey. But the **WILD** beauty of the countryside was worth the effort.

It was two o'clock in the afternoon, and

there was still plenty of **ROAD** ahead of them. Pamela's calculations might have been a bit too optimistic.

The **MOUSELETS** had almost made their way around Loch Duich when suddenly the weather got worse. A stinging rain started to fall. They stopped to discuss what to do next.

"My belly's **RUMBLING** louder than a souped-up sports car!" Pamela wailed, rubbing her stomach.

"And this **humidity** is a horror show for my fur!" cried Colette.

Violet frowned. She was so worried about Bridget she hated to stop. But the road was too wet to continue, so they had to make a **DETOUR**.

At the first crossroads, the mouselets turned left. Tired and **soaked**, they continued along the next road until they found themselves in front of something **spectacular**.

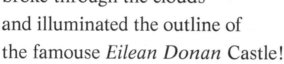

As quickly as it had started, the rain stopped. Sunlight broke through the clouds and illuminated the outline of the famouse *Eilean Donan* Castle!

The castle's dark **WALLS** and its stone bridge looked as though they were **SUSPENDED** between the clouds. The ancient building stood on a small island surrounded by three large **LAKES**. The water reflected the pearl gray sky like a mirror.

Paulina stopped and turned off her motorcycle's **engine**. The other mouselets did the same.

The Thea Sisters stood in silence, staring

at this **enchanting** place. They felt as though they had driven straight into a fairy tale.

Violet couldn't believe her **EYES**. To think that if it hadn't started to rain, they never would have seen this **splendid** sight!

After a few moments, Colette squeaked up. "Okay, sisters, this is pretty and all, but I'm **soaked** to the fur! Let's keep going."

The mouselets agreed. They continued on for another few miles and found a nearby

village where they could dry off and have a snack!

After a nice cup of **tea** and some delicious shortbread*, the five friends were ready to take off once more.

VROOM VROOM VROOOOOM!

At last, they reached Kyle of Lochalsh and crossed the Skye Bridge.

* Traditional Scottish cookies made with sugar, flour, and lots of butter!

"Hooray! We're on the Isle of Skye!" Nicky cheered once they'd set paw on the other side.

But there was no time to stop and celebrate. With Violet urging them on, the mouselets sped through Kyleakin, Broadford, and Portree. The street signs flew by **quickly**. The **THEA SISTERS** were getting closer to their destination.

The farther they went from the Scottish mainland, the **wilder** and more untouched the countryside became. There were no planted fields — just green moors dotted with purple heather and thistle **flowers**. Sparkling streams flowed down through the hills. Every so often, the mouselets would turn a corner and see cliffs that dropped off into the sea and a few fishermice's huts along the small bays.

At last, they came to a sign that read:

Finally, they had reached Bridget's village! When they caught **sight** of 𝔐ac𝔑amouse 𝔔astle on a cliff at the edge of the village, the Thea Sisters exchanged worried **LOOKS**: Would they find Bridget waiting for them?

𝔐ac𝔑amouse 𝔔astle

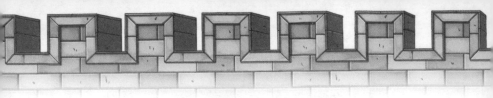

MACNAMOUSE CASTLE

MacNamouse castle was built on a cliff **OVERHANGING** the sea. It had a large tower on each side of the **lowered** drawbridge at the entrance. The tower on the right was in good shape, but the tower on the left showed deep **cracks**: Parts of the battlements had broken off and fallen into the moat below.

The Thea Sisters left their motorcycles in front of the castle, where several cars were already parked, and **crossed** the bridge on paw.

The castle's courtyard was deserted, but they could hear the **ECHO** of angry squeaking from above.

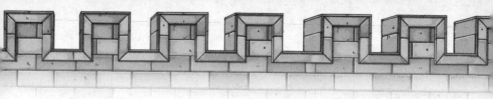

"Maybe the clan reunion has already started," Colette whispered.

"Let's go!" Paulina said, pointing to a **WOODEN** staircase that led up.

They scampered upstairs and knocked on a door that had faint **light** streaming from behind it. No one came to open it. From inside, though, they could distinctly hear **ARGUING**.

"YOU CAN FORGET IT, ANGUS! We're not turning this castle into an amousement park!"

"Oh, yeah?! Well, then I'm not giving a cent for the restoration! MacNamouse Castle will disintegrate into a pile of **rubble**."

The mouselets exchanged looks.

"Holey cheese! What a catfight," said Nicky, shaking her snout.

Pamela tried knocking **HARDER**. That

was when she realized that the door was slightly ajar.

"What should we do?" asked Colette.

Paulina **SHRUGGED**. "We didn't come all this way just to turn tail and head home."

Violet nodded. "That's right. Bridget needs us!"

So the Thea Sisters gathered up their

courage, pushed on the heavy door, and went in timidly.

"UM, excuse us?"

They found themselves in a large room **lit** only by candles. Right in front of them were two **big**, mean-looking ratlings. They were identical in every way, with bristly fur that was as yellow as a slice of American cheese. They quickly **BLOCKED** the mouselets' way.

"Who are you?!" the one on the right asked threateningly.

"Nosy tourists!" the other one said sharply. "This castle is private property! Get out! Scram!"

"But we're **FRIENDS** of Bridget MacNamouse," Violet replied faintly. "She asked us to come!"

"Bridget?!" the two rodents exclaimed.

"Finally! Bridget's here!" someone shouted from the back of the room.

"You've wasted a lot of time, mousey! **Shame on you!**" a grumpy voice croaked.

"In my day, we came on paw from the four corners of Scotland for clan meetings! And *no one* ever arrived late!" added a third squeak, which was LOUD and **SHRILL**.

The two rodents moved aside, and the Thea Sisters glimpsed the rest of the room. At the far end was a long, massive **WOODEN** table with lots of mice seated around it.

Violet stepped forward. "Bridget isn't with us! We were hoping to find her here."

An **old, THIN** rodent with a snout that was as **SHARP** as a cheese knife pounded his fist on the table. **Bam!!!**

"This is too much! Not only is Bridget

delaying our meeting, but she's invited strangers into the castle!"

An elderly rodent with SNOW-WHITE fur glanced at him. "Don't be so grouchy, Angus." Then she gave the mouselets an encouraging smile and gestured for them to come closer. "You're friends of Bridget, **my wee bairns***? Where did you come from?"

"We're her classmates at Mouseford Academy, on Whale Island!" Violet replied, SMiliNG back. "I'm Violet, and this is Pamela, Paulina, Nicky, and Colette."

The old mouse nodded **kindly**. "Welcome to MacNamouse Castle, mouselets! I am Lillian, Bridget's aunt. Everyone gathered here belongs to the 𝕸𝖆𝖈𝕹𝖆𝖒𝖔𝖚𝖘𝖊 clan. Don't be afraid. Come sit with us . . . and together let's figure out what could have happened to Bridget!"

43

* The Scottish way of saying "little ones."

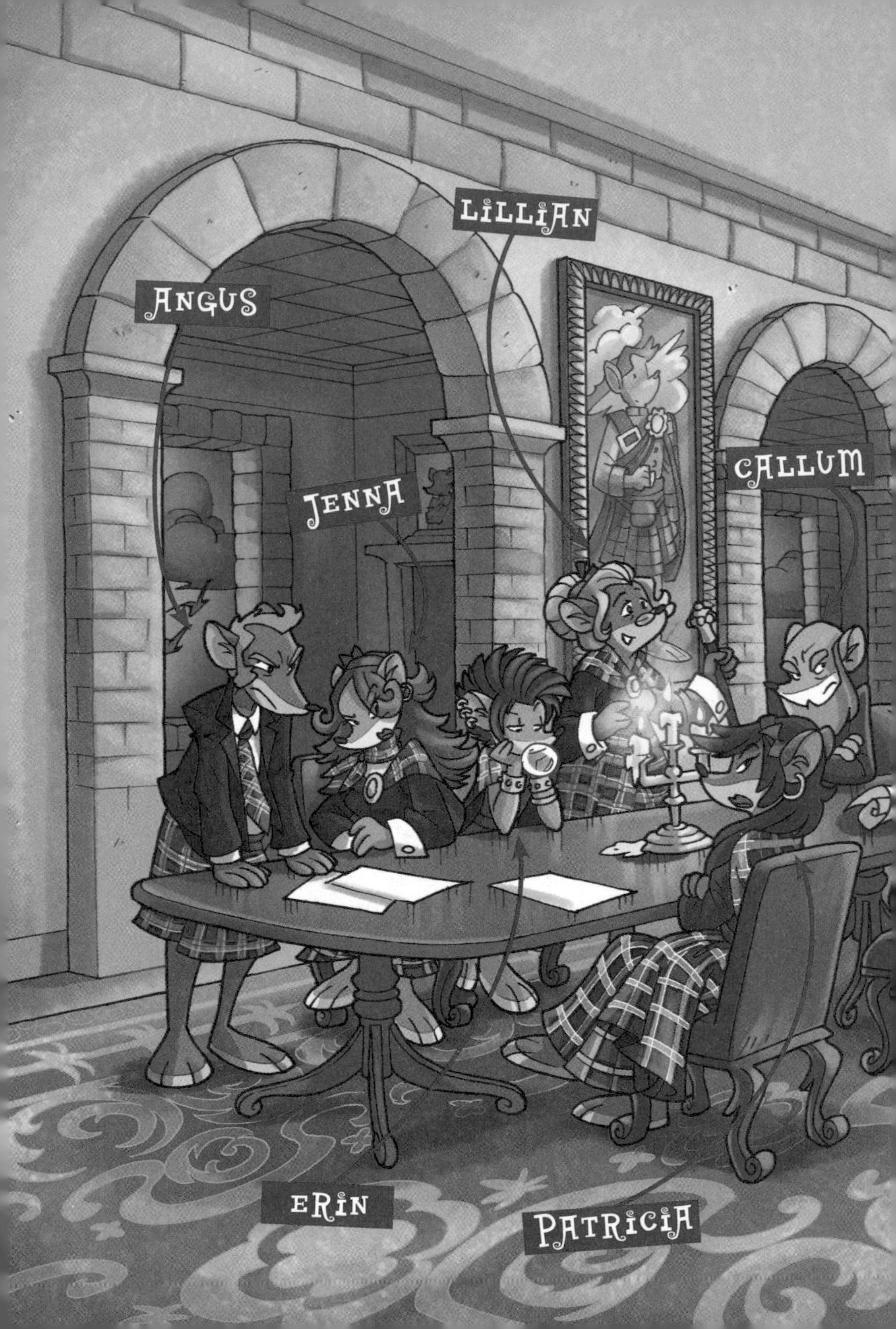
LILLIAN
ANGUS
JENNA
CALLUM
ERIN
PATRICIA

THE RULES
OF THE CLAN

All eyes were on the Thea Sisters as they explained the reason for their **TRIP**. Violet was the most *concerned*. "Bridget should have arrived days ago!" she exclaimed.

"Ah, but we haven't seen her here!" was the **hasty** reply from Liam and Connor, the two ratlings with bright yellow fur.

CLUE!

"THAT'S ENOUGH!"

Angus MacNamouse burst out. He was huffier than a wet cat in a rainstorm. "I'm a businessmouse, and I don't want to lose any more time. We only have three more days until the full moon. If Bridget doesn't arrive in time, we'll have to exclude her from the meeting. No exceptions for wee **BRATTY** mouselets!"

With that, he stomped out of the room. His sons Liam and Connor followed, hot on his **heels**.

Colette wasn't able to **HIDE** her disappointment. "But aren't you worried about your niece? If Bridget isn't here, something must have happened to her!"

"We Highlanders are tough rodents, and the rules of the 𝕸𝖆𝖈𝕹𝖆𝖒𝖔𝖚𝖘𝖊 clan are

Angus and his sons don't seem too worried about Bridget's disappearance! Is it possible they know where she is?

tough, too!" replied Orson, an ancient rodent with a long beard.

"You see, the clan meeting takes place on the first day of the full **MOON** and begins when all the clan members have arrived," Erin, the youngest, explained to the mouselets. "If someone doesn't show up, they're left out!"

"The **Highlanders** used to race to the meetings," said Orson. "Anyone who arrived late wasn't allowed to squeak!"

Lillian tried to *lighten* the atmosphere. "Come on, Orson. Maybe Bridget arrived without our noticing and has left some **TRACKS** in her room here at the castle!"

The Thea Sisters looked at one another. They were all thinking the same thing: They had to check out that room!

"Um, squeaking of Bridget's room, would you mind if we took a look?" Violet asked nervously.

"Of course not, my dears!" declared Lillian, although it was clear from the look on Orson's snout that he minded very much indeed.

Erin turned to them. "Our caretaker, Ewan, will take you there. It's **UPSTAIRS**."

At that, a young, energetic rodent

Follow me!

EWAN

with red fur scurried in. "Hi, everyone! I'm Ewan," he said **CHEERFULLY**, gesturing for them to follow him.

The Thea Sisters thought he was very pleasant and much different from Bridget's grouchy relatives!

"So you're friends of Bridget from **MOUSEFORD ACADEMY**, right?" Ewan asked as he led the mouselets along a **DARK** corridor and up a steep staircase. He held a FLASHLIGHT to light the way.

The young rodent seemed to want to chat. "Tell me, how does Bridget like the academy?

Is she **happy**? Does she have lots of friends?"

"She's very quiet," Violet responded. "But she certainly has friends: us!"

"We were hoping to find her here," Nicky added. "Since she left, we haven't had any **news** from her."

Ewan stopped short. "Hmm . . . that's strange! She knows how important the clan meeting is!"

At this point Pam couldn't hold back any longer. "Crusty **carburetors**! How come everyone knows what's being discussed in this meeting except us?!"

Ewan **BURST** out laughing. "Stick with me, mouselets! I'll explain a few things about the **MacNamouse** clan."

FAMILY PORTRAITS

As they made their way along the castle's long, dark hallways, Ewan filled the Thea Sisters in. "You see, my family has been working for the MacNamouses for centuries. My siblings and cousins and I all take turns coming here to take care of the **garden** and do maintenance. We do it for the sake of **tradition**, not for **LOVE** for the MacNamouses!"

"They seem like a very cranky bunch," Colette **OBSERVED**.

Ewan laughed. "You can **squeak** that again! They hate each other. They've been **FIGHTING** since the days of Ryan the Rough and Ethan the Spiteful! Now the future of the castle is at stake, and as always, the clan has **split** into two sides."

"Two sides?" Nicky inquired.

"Yes. The *traditionalists* want to keep the castle just as it's always been — closed to the public, unsafe, and without any comforts. There isn't even running **water** or electricity, as you can see!" Ewan explained, raising his flashlight.

Then he stopped. "Look! We're in just the right place to talk about the characters in this story."

Ewan and the mouselets were standing on the castle's impressive **STONE** staircase. The walls above them were covered in ancient portraits.

Ewan **shone** his flashlight on a large painting that had faded with age. "That's

ALISTAIR
MACNAMOUSE,
THE FOREFATHER

Alistair MacNamouse, the head of the clan that built this castle a thousand years ago! He was a **GREAT** leader who had a deep love for Celtic culture and traditions."

"This castle has been standing for a thousand years?!" asked Pamela, **AMAZED**.

Ewan nodded. "It's been rebuilt many times, but the oldest parts have been connected to the new ones."

Paulina **LOOKED** up at the second row of paintings. "What about those tiny portraits **up there**? Who are they?"

THE CELTS IN SCOTLAND

The Celts arrived in Scotland in the first millennium BC. They brought many of their traditions with them, including the use of iron. When the Romans reached Scotland for the first time, they called the ancient Celts *Picts* (from the Latin word for "painted"), possibly because of their many tattoos.

"Those are my ancestors!" Ewan replied, **blushing**. "Malcolm the Loyal was Alistair MacNamouse's squire. He followed him in all his ventures and saved his life many times. Since then, his descendants have **loyally** served the clan and taken care of the castle."

Ewan's chest swelled with **PRIDE** as he squeaked.

"Well, if you ask me, it seems like there's not much to say about Alistair MacNamouse's descendants!" Nicky commented.

Ewan **sighed**. "What you've heard is just the tip of the cheese slice! The other side of the family can't wait to **transform** the castle into some kind of amusement park, with lots of fake ghosts and spooky music."

The mouselets looked at one another with **ALARM**. This must be why Bridget was so worried!

"We must find Bridget," Ewan concluded. "The MacNamouses seem all too happy she's **FAR** away from this meeting!"

The Thea Sisters agreed. It was time to take action!

The MacNamouse clan is split into two opposing groups. It's possible that one of the groups doesn't want Bridget to participate in the meeting — but why?

TO MOLLY HOUSE!

Unfortunately, Bridget's room was EMPTY. She hadn't been there in months.

"Well, she may have made it back to the Isle of Skye, but she definitely hasn't been to the **castle**," said Violet.

"Perhaps she's staying with friends?" Pamela suggested.

"Squeaking of staying somewhere, we need to find a place to spend the **NIGHT**," said Nicky.

"Could you recommend a hotel in the village?" Paulina asked Ewan.

"Sure! You're in **LUCK**!" he replied. "There's only one place to spend the night in **OAKSMOUSE**:

CABOC

CHAPPIT TATTIES

BASHED NEEPS

APPLE CAKE

Molly House. And Molly just happens to be my mother!"

Half an hour later, the Thea Sisters had settled into the welcoming inn that belonged to Ewan's mother. Everyone was seated quite **comfortably** at a table in front of a **fragrant** plate of *Caboc* (cream cheese rolled in toasted oats) along with dishes of *chappit tatties* (mashed potatoes) and *bashed neeps* (thin-sliced turnips with beans).

"**Yum!** What a meal!" Pamela **exclaimed**, her cheeks full of **FOOD**.

"And it's not over yet!" Ewan replied, licking his whiskers. "Just wait until you taste my mother's specialty!"

"**Yum** . . . what is it?" Colette asked.

"Apple cake with custard, which is a **warm** vanilla sauce!" Ewan exclaimed.

The mouselets all sighed with anticipation. "We should stop eating now to leave some space in our bellies," Nicky said.

The welcoming atmosphere of the inn was as different as one could imagine from the damp **chill** of MacNamouse Castle. In the main dining room, a fire crackled brightly in the stone fireplace, and everyone was relaxed and smiling, happy to be passing the time with such **pleasant** company.

Ewan's brothers and sisters served the tables and helped their mother in the kitchen.

"You're not **giving** them a paw?" Paulina asked him.

The ratling **shook** his snout. "Not this week, because it's my turn at the castle!" Then he winked *MYSTERIOUSLY*. "But later on I'll help, too. You'll see!"

During dinner, Ewan squeaked a lot about Bridget with his new **FRIENDS**. "Bridget and I have known each other since we were wee mouselings. She's always been very s h y, so some people think she's snobby. But she's such a kind, sensitive mouselet."

Colette elbowed Pamela, who, taken by surprise, accidentally swallowed a big mouthful of *chappit tatties.*

"Hey!" Pam exclaimed. "What was that for?!?"

Colette gestured for her to lower her squeak. "Have you noticed how Ewan's

EYES light up whenever he talks about Bridget?!" she whispered **conspiratorially**.

Truth be told, Bridget was the only topic of conversation at their table. No one could think of anything else. Where could she be? Why hadn't they heard from her?

"Maybe she's staying with a friend in the area, like Pamela suggested," said Paulina. She was trying to reassure Ewan, whose expression had **darkened**.

"Of course! Why didn't I think of that

earlier?!" he exclaimed as his eyes filled with **HOPE**. "But tomorrow I have to return to the castle, so I won't be able to look for her."

"Leave it to us, Ewan," Nicky declared. "We'll do it! All we need is her friends' addresses."

Just then, one of Ewan's brothers called him from the kitchen. He scurried away.

A few moments later, the sound of bagpipes made everyone fall silent.

Ewan and his brothers came back into the room, singing a *sweet* song in an **UNFAMILIAR** language. It was an ancient Celtic ballad!

The mouselets smiled at one another as they listened. But then Violet grew serious again. Hearing this music made her **worry** about Bridget once more. Where could she be?

GREAT HIGHLAND BAGPIPE

The Great Highland Bagpipe, or *piob-mhór* ("great bagpipe" in Gaelic), is a traditional Scottish instrument and is considered a national symbol of Scotland. The bagpipe is a wind instrument made of a large leather bag, a chanter, a blowpipe, and three drones. The player creates the melody by blowing into the blowpipe and pressing different notes on the chanter. At the same time, the player leans on the bag with one elbow, which forces air through the chanter. Air is also forced through the drones, each of which has a single reed. Together, the drones create the deep, constant background sound that is the bagpipe's trademark.

CELTIC BALLADS

A ballad is a simple song that tells a story. Ballads often tell stories about events that really happened. Celtic ballads are famous because they often tell old fables and legends and have been passed orally from one generation to the next.

THE MACNAMOUSE TWINS

The next morning, Nicky **jumped** to her paws the moment her eyes opened. She was a morning mouse. "Wake up, sleepysnouts!" she called to her companions, who took a bit longer to get up. The motorcycle journey had **WORN** them out!

"Nicky, do you always have to be so cheerful in the morning?" Pamela groaned, pulling her covers up to her snout. "Some of us need a bit more **sleep**, thank you very much."

Violet scampered out of bed. "Nicky's right. We're here on a mission. Let's go, mouselets!"

A few minutes later, the Thea Sisters trooped down to breakfast, where they were

surprised to find Liam and Connor MacNamouse reading the newspaper.

Because of the twins' blond **fur**, the Thea Sisters had nicknamed them the golden grumps. When Violet greeted them, they replied with a polite . . . grunt!

But the mouselets had plenty of other things to think about, like the **delicious** breakfast Ewan's mother had prepared for them. **SLURP!**

While Paulina bit into a piece of apple pie, the others dove into bowls of oat porridge with cinnamon sugar, with crispy pastries on the side.

"They're called *Aberdeen rowies*, and they're eaten warm, with **butteR** and bitter-orange marmalade," Molly explained. **CLUE!** Then she nodded toward the twins and whispered, "Those two never come here for **BReakFast**. I think they must be here for you!"

"Hmm, interesting," Violet murmured.

"They're not worried about Bridget, so they must be keeping an **EYE** on us!" Nicky crossed her arms, **annoyed**. "I can't stand those two grouches, and I like their **dad** even less!"

"Ditto!" Colette agreed. "When we arrived last night, it was Angus who insisted on

Why are Liam and Connor watching the Thea Sisters? Could they have something to do with Bridget's disappearance?

starting the meeting without Bridget."

"Well, if they think they can stop the Thea Sisters, they're in for a **big** surprise!" Paulina **declared**.

"You said it, sister!" Pam agreed, jumping to her paws. "Let's **GO** grab our gear and jump onto our **MOTORCYCLES**.

I'd like to see those golden grumps try to hold us back!"

When the **mouselets** came back down from their rooms, Connor and Liam had disappeared.

Nicky shrugged. "Come on, mouselets! Let's go find Bridget's friends."

With a loud **rumble**, they headed out on their bikes. But they had to slow down right away, since the road along the coast was very **narrow**. It hugged the jagged coastline. The clouds in the sky were reflected by the dark ocean **WAVES**.

For long stretches, the road was wide enough for just one vehicle. If someone had been trying to go in the **opposite**

direction, the mouselets would have had to wait for them to pass. But the Thea Sisters didn't run into any problems that morning.

"Way to go, Pam!" Violet said admiringly. "Your motorcycle idea was pure genius!"

"*Double* genius!" Paulina agreed. "But, mouselets, we've got company! The twins' JEEP has been following us for a while. Let's lose those twerps!"

VRRROOOOM!

The mouselets gave it their all, but they weren't able to put much DISTANCE between them and the jeep.

"Hrm, those two know the island better than we do!" Nicky grumbled.

After a few more bends in the road, the mouselets found just the solution they were looking for: a flock of SHEEP!!!

A MOUSE IN SHEEP'S CLOTHING

As soon as Nicky saw the sheep in the pasture, she had a **FABUMOUSE** idea for getting rid of their pursuers.

While the others continued, she stopped her **MOTORCYCLE**. Then she started to shout at the flock, **waving her paws** to

herd the sheep. A few moments later, the flock was blocking the road.

When Liam and Connor's **JEEP** arrived, they had to slam on the brakes to avoid all those sheep. They kicked up a huge dust cloud!

Nicky hopped back on the motorcycle, and she and Violet took off at full speed, waving at their two followers.

Bye-bye!

The twins had no choice but to stay where they were, scratching their snouts.

A little bit **ahead**, the other two motorcycles had stopped to wait.

"Nicky, you're sharper than a block of cheddar!" Paulina cheered. Nicky blushed.

The mouselets resumed their ride. Soon they found themselves at a crossroads. At Pamela's signal, they hit the brakes, got off their motorcycles, and **hid** behind thick bushes in the woods. Then they waited.

A few minutes later, the twins' jeep took the road to the right and **zoomed** ahead.

"SMOKIN' SWISS CHEESE!" Pamela shouted triumphantly. "We've lost them!"

Now certain that they weren't being **FOLLOWED**, the Thea Sisters emerged from their hiding place and took the road on the left.

But just when they least expected it, an old van **BLOCKED** the middle of the road. There was no way to get past it!

An unfamiliar old rodent stood next to the van and stared at them with a **SOUR** look. It was difficult to say how old he was: There was a thick **CLUMP** of white fur between his ears, but his paws were solid on the ground, his back was straight, and his arms were as strong as a **YOUNG** rodent's.

Who could he be? An accomplice of the twins? Another member of the MacNamouse clan?

After he'd **examined** them one by one, the old rodent said, "So you're the famouse Thea Sisters! Well, it sure took long enough to get rid of those two **goons**. Come on, follow me!"

Then he got into the van and turned on the **engine**.

The mouselets were squeakless. They **exchanged** looks of confusion: Could they trust this strange rodent?

The old rodent noticed that they hadn't moved. He stuck his snout out the window and shouted, "Well, hurry up, then! *Bridget's waiting for you at the lighthouse!*"

TO THE LIGHTHOUSE!

When the Thea Sisters reached the lighthouse, a slim figure came to meet them. From far away, they could see only that this rodent was wearing denim **overalls** and a tartan beret.

A **HIGH** squeak greeted them — Bridget's! "Violet! Mouselets! **Welcome** to Fljot Point!"

Violet jumped off her motorcycle and ran to embrace her friend. The others joined in. They hugged Bridget tightly, peppering her with kisses and questions.

SMACK! SMACK! SMACK!

"What happened?"

"Why are you **HIDING**?"

"Why haven't you answered our calls?"

"We've been so worried about you!"

Bridget's big gray eyes filled with tears. "Mouselets, it was as **HORRIBLE** as Aunt Jenna's home-cooked haggis! It's my cousins' fault that I lost my cell phone. I barely managed to send a **text message**, but I was sure you'd come help me."

Bridget led the Thea Sisters inside the lighthouse, an old watchtower that had been turned into a home for its **guardian**. She introduced them to the rodent who had first met them when they arrived at the lighthouse. "This is Ben, guardian of the lighthouse, and a dear **FRiEND**."

With a wave of his paw, Ben invited the mouselets to enter the only room in the lighthouse. Inside, there were nets, fishing poles, and model ships. The only pieces of furniture were a long **WOODEN** bench and a rocking chair.

"Sean **MacNamouse**, Bridget's grandfather, was my best friend," **old** Ben explained. "In our youth, we shared many things, including a great **passion** for sailboats. When Sean grew tired of his clan's constant arguments, he would take refuge here in the lighthouse, with me and my bagpipe."

"That's why I turned to Ben at this **DANGEROUS** time," Bridget said, picking up Ben's tale. "When I got off the ferry, I found Liam and Connor waiting for me."

"The golden grumps!" the Thea Sisters exclaimed.

"**Ha! Ha! Ha!**" Bridget laughed. "What a perfect nickname! Yes, all I can say about my cousins is that the cheese doesn't fall far from the cracker. They wanted me to support Angus's idea to turn the castle into an amusement park!"

"What a **cat-astrophe**!" Ben declared, his eyes **GLITTERING** with indignation.

Bridget continued. "Liam insisted that I get in their jeep. *'Da wants you to be a guest at our house!'* he said."

"Guest?! Yeah, right!" Pamela snorted.

Bridget nodded. "That's just what I

thought! I knew that they wanted to keep me from participating in the meeting and from voting against them. The decision has to be unanimous, you see. So I ESCAPED. But there were two of them, and it wasn't easy to get away. I JUMPED onto a boat docked at the wharf. But just as I sent a text message to Violet, a WAVE rocked the ship and my cell phone fell into the sea! At least you received my call for help."

ANCIENT HISTORY

As she was listening to Bridget's story, Violet **suddenly** remembered something. "Bridget, before leaving the academy, you mentioned that you had a mission to complete. Can you tell us what you meant?"

Bridget **nodded**. "That's exactly why I asked for your help. I can't do it alone — there isn't enough time! Before I explain, you need to hear a bit of history: the ancient history of the 𝕸𝖆𝖈𝕹𝖆𝖒𝖔𝖚𝖘𝖊 clan!"

Then she turned to Ben, who sat in the **ROCKING** chair. "Do you want to tell it, Ben? No one knows it better than you."

Ben nodded, a serious look on his snout. "Alistair MacNamouse was a **STRONG** and courageous leader, but he also loved the culture and traditions of his people. So he called to his court the most **FAMOUSE** bard of that time, Jorg, to sing about the **ancient** Scottish heroes and preserve the memory of their deeds. Jorg was very loyal to Alistair and, just like Malcolm the Loyal, was always by his side. Thanks to his **ballads**, we still know many details of the history of the MacNamouses and their castle, like the story of the warriors' stones!"

"What are the warriors' **STONES**?" Colette whispered.

BARDS

Bards were ancient Celtic poets and storytellers. They were very important figures: Thanks to their ballads, stories of the deeds of Scottish heroes and the oldest Celtic legends have been handed down through the centuries.

Ben heard her question and began telling the story. "Long ago, before leaving for **BATTLE**, each Scottish warrior left a stone on the ground, **CARVED** with a symbol or a message. The stones formed a huge pile. When they returned from battle, each warrior picked up his stone. The warriors who didn't return were remembered by the stones they had left behind."

The Thea Sisters listened, *entranced*.

Ben continued. "Alistair MacNamouse used these **ancient** stones when he built his castle, placing them in particular spots so that they wouldn't be scattered. That way, there would always be a record of the warriors who hadn't returned from the last battle."

The mouselets hung on every last word. What a **FASCINATING** story!

"Alistair did not have direct descendants," the old guardian continued, "just two nephews, Ethan and Ryan, who were **jealous** of each other and always arguing. Alistair knew that with them in charge of the castle, the clan would always be arguing and fighting!"

"Unfortunately, he was right," Bridget sighed.

"According to **legend**," continued Ben, "on a winter's night, during a strong storm, Alistair placed a piece of parchment in Jorg's paws: It was his will! It contained the name of the heir of the castle and of the MacNamouse treasure!"

"But in the portraits of Ethan and Ryan in the gallery, they appeared together!" Pam observed. "So Alistair's will didn't name one heir, but two!"

"You're an excellent **OBSERVER**, Pamela," Ben said, "but actually, no one knows who was chosen as heir. And it wasn't necessarily one of the two nephews! Only Jorg knew the contents of the parchment, but after Alistair's death, he DISAPPEARED, taking his secret with him. Since no one knew what the will said, the two nephews assumed **POWER** together."

Bridget interrupted, **UPSET.** "My grandfather found some very old papers in the castle, signed by Jorg himself! They didn't contain the name of the heir. But they showed that Ryan and Ethan had tried to **DESTROY** their uncle's will so that they could secure the castle and the treasure for themselves."

"But why would they **DESTROY** it if it named one of them?" Paulina asked.

"An excellent question!" Ben agreed. "It almost makes me think it didn't name them. But we may never know for sure." He **shook** his snout. "Jorg escaped by **SEA**, followed by the two brothers. Before he went, he left his ballads as testimony of everything that had happened. Then he **HID** the will and the treasure in a place that only a true Highlander, **LOYAL** to tradition, would know how to find."

"So that's how Ethan and Ryan took over!" Nicky said, **INDIGNANT**.

"Well, they tried," Bridget replied. "Ethan and Ryan took over the title, but they never stopped **arguing** and getting in each other's way. And that's how it's been for all the MacNamouse descendants . . . even today!"

"So your **MISSION** is to find the lost will," Violet guessed.

Bridget **SMILED**, pleased. "I knew you'd understand!"

BRiDGET'S miSSiON

Ben and Bridget's story explained a lot. But Nicky was still a little perplexed. "After years and years of this family feud, it's a miracle that the castle hasn't fallen into ruins!"

Bridget's **expression** softened. "It's all thanks to Malcolm's descendants, who have always taken care of the castle with love and dedication! Ben is one of them."

"And we've met another one!" Colette interrupted. "A very cute ratling named Ewan."

"Ewan is my oldest grandson," Ben said. "He doesn't know that Bridget's with me. I

didn't want him to have to keep the secret while he's with the MacNamouses at the castle."

"Yes, Ewan is a very honorable mouse," said Bridget. "He always carries out the **clan's** traditions." She was **blushing** from the tips of her WHiSKeRS to the tip of her tail! Colette winked at Pamela **MISCHIEVOUSLY**.

Violet, on the other paw, was all business. "So what's our next step?"

"Come with me!" Bridget said, leading them upstairs. The mouselets found

themselves in a room without a ceiling. There was a very long staircase shaped like a **snail**. It curled up and up, all the way to the top of the lighthouse, where there was a room filled with **BOOKS**, files, and boxes of documents.

"This place is a **bookworm's** dream!" Paulina exclaimed.

"My grandfather was a student of history," Bridget explained. "He got sick of the clan's constant bickering, and he was determined to find out once and for all who was the legitimate owner of the castle."

Bridget stroked the cover of an **old** book. "These are all the documents that he collected. He left them to me when he passed away. Now I only have two days to find the answer, which is why I need your help!"

Pamela's eyes **widened**. "You want us to read *all this stuff*?!"

Bridget laughed and **shook** her snout. "Of course not! According to my grandfather, Jorg hid the will in the castle. I need to keep researching here, but it would be great if you could take a look around the castle. Jorg was famouse for his ballads, but also for his sharp wit and his **RIDDLES**. Maybe he left some kind of clue."

"Sure thing, sister!" Pam exclaimed, **relieved**. "Sounds like a good plan to me! You and Ben take the books, and we Thea Sisters will take action!"

Everyone **burst** out laughing. Old Ben was **beaming**; he was delighted to see that Bridget had found such devoted friends.

THE BALLAD OF THE THREE STONES

While Bridget stayed at the lighthouse to sift through her grandfather's documents, the Thea Sisters returned to Molly House.

As soon as the mouselets scurried in the door, Ewan **RAN** to meet them. "Have you found Bridget?! I was starting to get worried about you, too!"

He does like her!

Thank goodmouse! Bridget's okay!

"We've got good news!" Violet responded. As soon as Ewan heard that Bridget was okay, he SmiLED from ear to ear.

The mouselets were starving after their day of adventure. Fortunately, Molly had made a wonderful barley soup for dinner.

"**Yum!**" cried Pam as she rubbed her belly after the meal. "That was whisker-licking good!"

After dinner, the inn's guests laughed and chatted. Some even started to *dance*! Ewan led the Thea Sisters in a Scottish jig that made their paws prance and their fur fly.

"**WHEEW!**" Paulina gasped after the final spin. "What a workout!"

Then Ewan put on some slow, sweet, sad music, and his sister Lizzy began to sing an ancient Celtic ballad.

The Thea Sisters clapped **enthusiastically**.

EVERYONE ON THE FLOOR!

A Scottish country dance is a traditional dance that's performed in groups of couples. The dancers line up in two rows, and several couples take a turn performing their steps. When those couples are done, a new batch of couples takes its turn.

"Can you translate it for us, Ewan?" Violet asked as the ratling plopped down next to them with a **cold** drink.

"It's called *The Ballad of the Three Stones*," Ewan explained, his eyes **shining**. "It was written by Jorg the Bard in the time of 𝕬𝖑𝖎𝖘𝖙𝖆𝖎𝖗 𝕸𝖆𝖈𝕹𝖆𝖒𝖔𝖚𝖘𝖊, actually! It goes something like this. . . ."

CLUE!

The castle walls hold three stones:
The stone that squeaks, the stone that cries, and the stone that fishes.
The stones can be opened with a flower,
By one who truly wishes.

Ewan **SHRUGGED**. "No one knows what it means. And lots of rodents have tried to figure it out!"

Jorg the Bard loved riddles. Could the words of his ballad have a hidden meaning?

THE MYSTERIOUS TAPESTRY

The next morning, the Thea Sisters headed up to the castle bright and early. They had made arrangements with Ewan: The ratling would let them in, but then he had to go work in the garden.

"Don't worry about us, Ewan," Paulina said, **REASSURING** him. "We'll see you later! We have a guidebook with information on the castle. We'll be fine."

The mouselets were just deciding where to begin when Angus appeared in front of them, accompanied by Liam and Connor.

"Good, good, **LOOK** who's here: Bridget's **friends**!" Angus observed with a nasty **SMILE**. "But what a shame that my delightful

niece still hasn't arrived! And the moment for the clan's decision is drawing near."

Pam looked like she was about to burst out with a sassy retort. Colette had to put a paw on her shoulder to **restrain** her. The Thea Sisters didn't want to reveal Bridget's plan!

"Yes . . . yes!" Connor ꜱɴɪᴄᴋᴇʀᴇᴅ. "Something tells me that our da's plan is going off without a hitch! Ha-ha!"

"Well, if that's the case, we'd like to visit

the castle while it's still standing," Violet replied **coldly**.

Angus looked like he wanted to *throw* them out, but Bridget's aunt Lillian stopped him. "That's a request we can't refuse! For our clan, **HOSPITALITY** is sacred!"

Angus chewed his whiskers. But he couldn't argue with his sister. So he insisted that a **family** member tag along with the mouselets.

"Erin will accompany them!" he declared with a **LOOK** that definitely didn't mean anything good. "She'll keep a close eye . . . I mean, she'll show them all the most interesting parts of the castle."

Erin, Bridget's cousin, was the youngest of the MacNamouses. As soon as she arrived, she exchanged **SCHEMING** looks with Angus. It was clear whose side she was on!

"With Erin hanging around, we won't be

able to look for the will," Paulina whispered.

Pam shook her snout sadly. "She's going to stick to us closer than a glue trap. I can tell."

Erin lazily led them to a brightly **LIT** room on the second floor.

"How **BEAUTIFUL**!" Violet exclaimed, noticing a tapestry that covered the entire back wall.

"Ugh, it's so *old-fashioned*!" Erin muttered.

The tapestry featured knights and ladies from another time. They were dancing amid gardens and F|✿W≡RiNG trees.

"It's strange, that **garden**," Violet noted.

"The hedges remind me of something, but I'm not sure what."

Paulina leaned in to take a closer look at the **pattern**. "You're right, Violet!" She pulled out her guidebook. "This must be what you're thinking of!" she exclaimed. "The garden in the tapestry is actually a map of the castle!"

"Really?!" Erin asked, suddenly curious.

Colette realized that this would be a good time to **distract** her.

"Um, are there any historical clothes in the castle?" she asked, taking Erin by the paw. "I don't really like old tapestries, but I *adore* those big gowns from long ago. You know, the ones with all the *lace*!"

Erin turned away from the tapestry. "Absolutely! There are whole wardrobes full!"

"Oooh, can I see them? And maybe try some on?" Colette begged. She sounded genuinely **enthusiastic**, but as she squeaked, she cast a sneaky look at her friends.

Nicky got in on the **ACT**. "Me, too! Me, too!" she cried. Then she whispered to Pam, "We'll keep her busy for a while. You three start looking for that will!"

THE STONE THAT
SQUEAKS

Once Erin, Nicky, and Colette had scurried off, Violet gazed at the tapestry. "The castle walls hold three stones: the stone that squeaks, the stone that cries, and the stone that fishes," she **mumbled**.

"What?" Pam asked. "I can't hear you, Vi."

"Those are the words to *The Ballad of the Three Stones*, remember?" Violet replied thoughtfully. She pointed to the tapestry's **pattern**. "Look at that mouse . . . she's fishing!"

"You're right!" Pam agreed. "And **look** at that one:

It looks like she's squeaking!"

"And this one is **crying**!" added Paulina, pointing to a third mouse. *"Just like the three stones in the ballad!"*

"My grandfather Chen always says, 'When too many coincidences pile up, perhaps they are not coincidences!'" Violet said solemnly.

Paulina compared the tapestry to the **MAP** of the castle and drew three **X**s that corresponded to the positions of the three mice. "The **mouse who squeaks** must be in the kitchen," she said at last. "The mouse who cries

MacNamouse Castle

is in the ruined tower, and the **third** . . . well! She must be outside the castle."

"So let's start in the kitchen," Pamela suggested. "It's the easiest to **FIND**!"

The kitchen was a big stone room with two large **FIREPLACES** and copper pans of various sizes hanging on the walls.

The three Thea Sisters spread out. Pamela

peeked out a window that overlooked the vegetable garden. Big black clouds warned of the arrival of a **STORM**.

Paulina inspected the two fireplaces to see if anything was hidden there.

Violet poked around in the clay pots and the sacks leaning against the wall. They contained **FLOUR**, potatoes, and other kinds of **FOOD**. Behind them, she noticed a marble plaque. "Hey, **mouselets**, help me move these sacks!"

On the wall was a tablet carved with the heads of **ANIMALS** with their mouths open, as if they were squeaking.

"**The Stone that Squeaks!**" Paulina exclaimed. Then a look of alarm crossed her snout. "We don't need to move it, do we?"

The **STONE** was cemented to the wall. There was no way the mouselets could

MOVE it without a chisel and some serious muscle power.

"Well, if the will is hidden there, we'll have to find a way to open it!" Pamela replied. She pulled at the piece of the stone that stuck out most: a bronze thistle flower set in the center.

"Maybe under here— **OOF!** —there's an opening," Pam suggested.

She gave it her all, but the stone didn't *move* an inch.

"It's **stuck** like a trap on the tail!" she sighed.

THE PARCHMENT

Violet pondered the situation. "What if we used some butter to grease the sides of the STONE? There's got to be some here in the kitchen!"

"In the cellar, for sure," Paulina said. She **scampered** down to the basement.

Sure enough, there was a huge package of butter in the basement pantry. The mouselets sliced off a generous pat and rubbed it all over the bronze FL✾WER.

As soon as the stone was good and greasy, Violet pressed on it, trying to ʃlidε it upward. After a moment or two, something clicked.

CLANK!

The center of the stone opened like a little

door, **revealing** a compartment carved into the marble. There was **something** inside!

Violet reached in and carefully pulled out a small, **ANCIENT** box.

"By cheese, I think you've got it!" cried Paulina, *excitedly*.

Violet and Paulina opened the box carefully. Inside lay a single sheet of parchment!

Violet immediately started to read it, but her **SMILE** quickly faded. "It's not Alistair's will."

"How can you tell?" Pamela asked, disappointed. She leaned over her friend's shoulder, **STRUGGLING** to decipher the **JAGGED** and **smudged** pawwriting.

"Because it's signed 'Jorg the Bard,'" Violet noted.

Paulina pointed out several names on the document. "**LOOK** here! I see the names Alistair, Ethan, and Ryan. . . . They're the mice from the story Ben told us!"

"So now we need to **LOOK** for the other stones from the ballad," Pam concluded.

She had just finished squeaking when the door to the kitchen **burst** open, and Liam and Connor stomped in.

"Uh, hi," said Violet, trying to hide the parchment behind her tail.

But it was too late. The twins had seen it. Before the mouselets could stop them, Liam had pushed Pam and Paulina into the **cellar** while his brother had ripped the parchment out of Violet's paws and dragged her after her friends.

The mouselets struggled to escape, but it was no use. The twins were too **strong**.

"Rat-munching rattlesnakes, what do you think you're doing?!" cried Paulina.

"You're messing with the wrong mice," Pam warned them. "You'll be sorrier than a cat in a dog kennel by the time we're through with you!"

"Shut your snout!" Liam cried. He *tied* up the three friends and gagged them. Then Connor took their **cell phones** and he and Ethan left, bolting the cellar door behind them.

Upstairs, the twins immediately called

Angus to tell him about the parchment. Liam and Connor were each as **huge** as overweight tabby cats, but they weren't very bright, and they didn't **dare** do a thing without their father's permission.

Angus listened to the horrible things his sons had done without batting a whisker. But when he heard about the parchment, he **JUMPED**. "Well, what does it say, you cheeseheads?"

"I don't know, **DA**. . . . It doesn't make sense!" Connor replied.

Angus immediately concluded that it must be the lost will. "**BURN IT**! And keep those busymice quiet until the end of the meeting. I'm certainly not going to let some silly will **ruin** my plan!"

LIKE RODENTS IN A MOUSETRAP!

Meanwhile, Colette, Erin, and Nicky were busy doing a period fashion show! What had started as a distraction was turning out to be kind of **fun**.

Inside old **CHESTS** and wardrobes, the mouselets had discovered satin ribbons, velvet gowns, feathered hats, and silk shawls.

Colette, Erin, and Nicky were trying on outfits and chattering away like old friends.

That was when Liam and Connor **SWOOPED** into the room. They pounced on Nicky and Colette and tied them up with some old wool scarves.

"What are you two cheddarfaces doing?! Has the cheese slipped off your cracker?!?" Erin **SHRIEKED** at her two cousins.

"Shut your trap, Erin!" Connor snapped.

"If we want your opinion, we'll let you know!" Liam snarled.

After they **GAGGED** Colette and Nicky and took their cell phones, the twins threw them in the cellar with Pamela, Paulina, and Violet.

The five mouselets looked at each other sadly. What next?

Meanwhile, Angus had decided that there was no time to lose. The clan meeting needed to happen right away, before anyone could discover what his sons had done with the Thea Sisters.

Now the majority is on my side, the **old** rodent thought. *But if Bridget arrives, who knows what might happen?*

No more delays!

More **determined** than ever, Angus joined the members of the clan in the Great Hall. "No more delays!" he cried. "We've already waited too long. We're not **LEAVING** here without making a decision!"

"But there's still one more day until the full **moon**!" Lillian protested.

"Yes, but there are new **cracks** in the tower!" Angus lied shamelessly. "If we don't start renovations right away, this castle will **collapse** on top of us!"

Outside, the wind was gusting. A stinging **rain** started to beat against the windows.

Ewan came in from the **garden** and started looking for the Thea Sisters. He was hoping they had discovered something.

After **WANDERING** through half the castle and finding no trace of the mouselets, he suddenly came across Liam and Connor, who were slipping out of the kitchen with **SNEAKY** looks on their snouts.

Ewan waited till they were out of sight. Then he rushed into the kitchen. "Colette! Nicky! Pamela! Paulina! Violet! Are you in here?!?"

NOT EVERYTHING BURNED!

The kitchen was quiet and empty. But Ewan glanced into the fireplace and noticed that something had been BURNED. He poked around between the flames with the fire tongs, but all he found were ashes.

He was about to leave when . . . THUMP!

A loud thumping sound came from the cellar.

"Is someone there?!" Ewan SHOUTED.

THUMP! THUMP!

Down in the cellar, the Thea Sisters, still bound and gagged, had heard him calling. They were banging their paws against the wall in a desperate attempt to get his

attention. After a moment or two, the cellar door flew open.

"M M M P F !" Pam whimpered.

"Pamela!" Ewan exclaimed, astonishcd. "Nicky! Violet! Paulina! Colette! What are you doing here, wrapped up like balls of fresh mozzarella?!" He hurried over and started untying them.

As soon as her mouth was free, Nicky *gasped*, "It was those terrible twins!"

"Yes, the two grouches, Liam and Connor!"

Violet grunted, **pulling** off the gag.

"After this experience, I think we can safely upgrade them from grumps to slimy sewer rats," said Paulina, rubbing her **sore** ankles.

"We had just found one of Jorg's parchments," Violet explained. "But they took it and . . ."

"They **BURNED** it in the fireplace!" Ewan finished for her. "I saw it there. Now it's just ashes, unfortunately!"

"It's not right!" Colette moaned, **shaking** her snout.

"Not *everything* has burned, Colette," Paulina said. "We still have two **STONES** to find. Maybe one is hiding the will!"

"We must find it before they know we're free!" Nicky declared.

Ewan was **baffled**. "*Stones?!* What are you squeaking about?"

"There's no time to explain!" Pam cried. "We'll tell you everything on the **WAY**. Where are the other stones, Paulina?"

Paulina pulled the guidebook out of her pocket and looked around for a bit of LIGHT. "If I remember right . . . Yes! We need to **CLIMB** the tower!"

Let's go find the other two stones!

THE STONE THAT
CRIES

All the members of the **MacNamouse** clan (except Bridget) were in the Great Hall, so none of them knew about the six shadows **SLINKING** along the corridor. The discussion was very heated, and Angus's squeak could be heard above the others, even through the thick castle walls.

"Bridget's right. Her relatives don't do anything but **argue**," Violet whispered.

"Follow me!" Ewan said. "I know a shortcut!"

The ratling knew all the castle's corridors and passageways like the back of his paw. The little group reached the tower in no time.

The **WOODEN** staircase that led to the top of the tower was very narrow, and the stairs **creaked**. The howling **WIND** blew in through the many cracks in the old stone.

"**Brrrrrrrrr!**" Colette whispered to Nicky. "This place is creepier than Count Ratula's crypt!"

Nicky nodded. "The **WHOLE** tower's crumbling like a house of cheese crackers! Here, hold my paw."

Once they reached the top, Violet took **CHARGE**. "Okay, let's start **LOOKING**, everyone! Remember,

CREAK CREAK

we need to find a stone of a mouselet who's crying."

As heavy rain beat down on the tower roof, the mouselets ran their paws over every inch of the stone wall around them.

After a few minutes, Nicky **shook** her snout in disappointment. "There's nothing that looks like a rodent crying up here."

"But there *must* be!" Paulina replied. "The tapestry clearly **POINTED** to this spot!"

"You're right," said Pam. "And we found the other stone right where the map said it would be. Let's keep looking."

All six mice began to **examine** the stones one more time. But it was no use: They all looked the same!

Suddenly, there was a flash of LIGHTNING above them, and the tower shook.

CRAAAAACK!

The lightning illuminated one of the windows right in front of Violet. She couldn't believe her **EYES**: Just outside the window was a stone in the shape of a mouse!

Violet called the others over and carefully approached the window.

A gargoyle* shaped like a female rodent was sticking out from the tower wall. Because of the rain, it looked like tears were rolling down her snout!

* A gargoyle covers the mouth of a drainpipe and is usually carved in the shape of an animal.

"The stone that cries!" Colette **CHEERED**.

"Hooray!" cried the other mouselets.

After finding the first STONE in the kitchen, the Thea Sisters knew what to look for: a mechanism made of bronze and shaped like a thistle FL✿WER.

"Here!" Pam cried all of a sudden. "Look! There's a carving of a thistle under the ledge."

Ewan **PUSHED** on the mechanism,

which was a little **RUSTY** after several centuries, and . . .

CLANK!

The bronze flower moved upward, and part of the ledge opened. Beneath it was a compartment that held an **ancient** box. Inside the box was another parchment!

"It must be the will!" Ewan declared. "That's the MacNamouse coat of arms next to Alistair's signature!"

"Quick, let's move those paws!" Nicky urged the group. "We need to show this to Bridget!"

As they scurried down the tower stairs, Violet *peeked* out the window and caught a GLIMPSE of a car approaching the castle. It was the police! But who could have called them?

WEE-OWW! WEE-OWW! WEE-OWW!

HELP IS HERE!

A few hours before, Bridget had tried to reach Violet on the phone. She was very worried. She hadn't heard any **news** from the Thea Sisters, and she was sure their silence meant they were in trouble.

Bridget tried every one of the mouselets' numbers, but their **cell phones** just kept ringing and ringing. After pacing back and forth **nervously** for a while, Bridget gathered up her courage and decided to go to the castle.

Why aren't they answering?!

She had to find out what had happened to her friends.

"Bridget, I'm not letting you go alone!" Ben said. "I'm sure those five **mouselets** are in trouble. We need help!"

Ben used his two-way radio to notify the Oaksmouse **POLICE**. "I've known all the policemice since they were wee bairns only this high. I know they'll do me a **favor**!"

Meanwhile, in the **Great Hall** of **MacNamouse Castle**, the arguing suddenly ground to a halt. Angus was winning the day, and now the clan just needed to vote by a **show** of paws.

There wasn't much doubt about what the ancient castle's fate would be. In the end, even the last undecided rodents gave in to Angus.

"So . . . ," the old rodent concluded

THREATENINGLY. "Who here agrees with my proposal to turn the castle into a modern amousement park? Raise your paws!"

Just then, the door flew open and Bridget burst into the room. She was **angrier** than a cat with a bad case of fleas. Two policemice were right behind her.

"Where are the Thea Sisters?" Bridget shouted. "What have you scoundrels done to my friends?!"

Where are the Thea Sisters?

Her arrival had an **AMAZiNG** effect. Angus's snout turned as pale as mozzarella. He STARED at her in disbelief. Liam and Connor turned bright red, as if they were sitting on the hot coals that had **burned** the parchment.

"Bridget, my deeeeeear!" Aunt Lillian chirped happily. She ran toward her niece with open paws. "Finally, you're here . . . and just at the right moment!"

Bridget gave her aunt a quick **HUG**, but she had more important matters to attend to. She turned to her uncle Angus. "Violet, Nicky, Paulina, Pamela, and Colette came to the castle. I'm sure of it. So where are they?"

Then she POINTED at Liam and Connor. "Where are my friends? Why haven't they answered my calls?"

"How should I know?!" Liam replied,

shrugging. He cast a nervous **LOOK** at the policemice behind her.

"They got tired of looking at **old** clothes, so they left!" Connor declared. "Isn't that right, Erin? Tell them!"

"Um . . . y-yes," Erin **stammered**. Her fur turned redder than a golden hamster's. "They got tired of looking at all our old junk. That French mouse said it was **moldier** than Brie on a baguette."

MYSTERY REVEALED!

Bridget didn't believe a word her cousins squeaked. She was more **DETERMINED** than ever to uncover the truth. So she turned to the two **POLICEMICE**. "We must look for them, *quickly*! I'm sure something dreadful has happened to them. They must be trapped somewhere in the castle!"

"Bridget, **stop** this nonsense at once!" Angus thundered. "I won't allow you to make **ACCUSATIONS** like that! And I will

never agree to let them search my cast —"

Before he could finish, though, his squeak was drowned out by a happy shout:

"BRIDGET! WE FOUND IT!"

With a blast of wind and rain, the Thea Sisters and Ewan scampered into the hall.

Violet led the group. She was **overjoyed** as she threw herself into Bridget's paws. "We found it! We found it!"

WE FOUND IT!

Liam and Connor **MOVED** toward her, gnashing their teeth, but the other mouselets **BLOCKED** their path.

"**Paws off!**" Pam ordered the two troublemakers.

"You'd better not touch a whisker on any of us!" Nicky added.

"You cheeseheads burned the wrong parchment! Ha-ha!" Colette **chuckled**.

The policemice came forward. "Are these your friends, Bridget? What have they found?"

Violet cleared her throat and held up the parchment **triumphantly**. *"The will of Alistair MacNamouse!"*

A **MURMUR** of amazement rippled through the group. Violet pawed the will to Aunt Lillian, who **examined** it closely.

There was a long pause. Then Lillian

squeaked, "Without a doubt, this is Alistair's will! And look . . . it says that the legitimate heir of the castle is . . ."

All the MacNamouses held their breath.

"Malcolm the Loyal and his descendants!"

Shouts of **amazement** and disbelief echoed through the hall.

Ewan was astounded.

Bridget was beaming with **happiness**.

"Oh, Ewan!" She clapped her paws. "Grandfather would be so pleased!"

The Thea Sisters **celebrated** enthusiastically. **"HOORAY! WOO-HOO!"**

Alistair couldn't

have chosen better: Only Malcolm's descendants had shown the **courage**, the loyalty, and the love for tradition that Alistair MacNamouse wanted on his land!

Angus was **LIVID**. He lunged at Lillian and tried to **SNATCH** the will from her paws. "It can't be! It's not valid!"

But Ewan was *quicker* than a cat with

a ball of yarn. He leaped across the room and **TACKLED** Angus!

"That's right, Ewan!" Pam cried, clapping. "You show him who's the boss now!"

The two policemice quickly intervened. The first officer pawcuffed Angus while the second made him hand over the parchment. "Whether the will is valid or not will be decided by a judge. For now, we'll take it!"

JUSTICE IS SERVED

The Thea Sisters' **MISSION** was complete. And so was Bridget's! The castle and all its assets would soon be officially turned over to Ben, the most direct heir of Malcolm the Loyal.

The Thea Sisters hurried to the lighthouse with Bridget and Ewan to share the wonderful news with the old WATCHMOUSE, who was surprised and delighted.

The mouselets organized a party to celebrate. Ewan's mom made delicious things to eat, and his siblings sang *traditional* Scottish songs all night. It was an unforgettable evening.

As the celebration began to wind down, the Thea Sisters, Bridget, Ewan, and

old Ben gathered around a big round table.

"It's a shame we never found the last STONE!" Paulina sighed.

Violet tried to cheer her up. "Well, to be honest, we don't know exactly where to look."

But Paulina couldn't stop thinking about it. She picked up the map of the castle with the three spots marked on it. "The third mark points to the cliff, **DOWN THERE** behind the castle."

"But there's nothing there but water!" Bridget replied, **confused**.

"Who knows what that third stone is hiding?" said Nicky, shrugging.

Bridget **smiled**. "You'll see. Ben will find out once he's the official owner of the castle!"

"No, thank you!" he replied. "I wouldn't leave my lighthouse for any **Castle** in the **world**! Ewan can move into 𝕸𝖆𝖈𝕹𝖆𝖒𝖔𝖚𝖘𝖊 𝕮𝖆𝖘𝖙𝖑𝖊 if he wants."

Ewan **JUMPED**. "What did you say?! Me?!"

Ben nodded. "You're young, and you've got more sense in your snout than all the MacNamouses put together!" A **sly** smile spread across his snout. "And maybe one day, you'll have Bridget by your side!"

Ewan and Bridget both **BLUSHED**. Ben's suggestion had **CAUGHT** them by surprise.

"Hooray for Bridget! Hooray for Ewan!" Colette cried enthusiastically, clapping her paws.

"Hooray for Bridget and Ewan!" the other Thea Sisters shouted together.

clap! clap! clap! clap! clap!

Bridget and Ewan looked at each other shyly. Ewan took Bridget's paw in his own.

"Now, don't get too excited, my dear!" Ben interrupted. "The castle needs lots of renovations, which require a lot of work. And renovations and work mean **MONEY**!"

Ewan sighed. His spirits **sank** at the thought of it.

ONE LAST ADVENTURE

It was time for the Thea Sisters' **adventure** on the Isle of Skye to come to a close. The mouselets had to return to **MOUSEFORD ACADEMY,** and so did Bridget.

"Not so fast! We still have one day left!"

Pam protested, crossing her arms.

Colette sighed and batted her eyelashes. "Let's at least give Ewan and Bridget some time to talk!"

"**GOOD IDEA!**" Violet and Paulina agreed.

Nicky, on the other paw, had just one goal in mind: getting a *move* on!

"I don't know about you," she said, "but ever since I saw the **RAPIDS** on this island, I've wanted to go kayaking!"

That night at dinner, Nicky asked Ewan where they could rent kayaks. She was determined to organize a *fun* outing for their last day.

Bridget gladly joined the group. The next morning, all seven mice set off for the riverbank. They were equipped with helmets, life vests, and **double-layered** waterproof jackets.

They rowed with paddles until they reached the point where the river began. After that, they took the whole course at supersonic **SPEEEEEEEEEEED**!

The current carried the kayaks forward along the narrow, **winding** stream. Bridget, Colette, Ewan, Nicky, Pamela, Paulina, and

Violet raced through rapids, jumps, and BUBBLING waterfalls.

Nicky was **crazy** about kayaking. Even Ewan, who was a real expert on the river, had a hard time keeping up with her!

Pam wasn't as skilled with boats or paddles as she was with **engines**, but she managed to keep her kayak from capsizing in the waves.

Colette, who was sitting behind Nicky, and Violet, who was sitting behind Ewan, quickly gave up on paddling. They just **GRIPPED** the sides of their kayaks to keep from flying out and shut their eyes tightly so they wouldn't have to watch!

Bridget and Paulina were the true wonders of the trip, though. They made their way **calmly**, paddling in perfect harmony.

At the end of the **course**, the stream

flowed into the sea. The four kayaks floated close to the island's high cliffs, right behind MacNamouse Castle. At that moment, the tide was particularly low.

Paulina pointed to a stone arch that was barely distinguishable from the rocky SURFACE. "What's that down there?"

Violet leaned over to get a better look. "It looks like some kind of entrance right at the WATER'S surface."

"But it can't be," Bridget replied. "There's nothing but ROCKS down there!"

"And yet . . . ," Ewan wondered aloud, quickly rowing over so that he could SEE it up close. "It's definitely an arch! It's not a natural opening. Let's go look!"

THE STONE
THAT FISHES

It was a big arch, and the kayaks passed through it without any **trouble**.

The Thea Sisters and their friends made their way into a cave carved out of **rock**. The floor sloped down toward the water, so the top half was dry. The rodents clambered out of their kayaks and continued on paw.

At the back of the cave, there were a tunnel and a **STAIRCASE** with steps carved into the wall.

"Where are we?" Bridget whispered.

The staircase came to an end in a small room full of cobwebs. It was narrow and **cramped**, with a strong odor of sea salt and **mold**. The only entrance was the way they had come in. You could get to the cave only by **SEA**.

"It's a secret hiding place," Pamela said.

"Also a place for fishing **equipment**, I guess," Paulina added, pointing at a pile of moldy fishing **NETS**.

Violet brushed away an **enormouse** cobweb and moved closer to the wall.

"Hey! *The stone that fishes!*" she exclaimed.

On the wall was a large marble plaque **DECORATED** with carvings of fish. In its center was a bronze thistle.

"The third stone! I can't believe it!" Paulina squealed with *excitement*. "Let's open it, quickly!"

Ewan grabbed the thistle flower tightly, and after a bit of a **STRUGGLE**, the mechanism finally clicked open.

This time, it wasn't just a tiny compartment that opened up, but the whole stone. Behind it lay an ancient chest.

The seven young rodents **gazed** at it in astonishment. It was so quiet you could hear a cheese slice drop.

After a moment, Ewan yanked at the padlock that kept the chest shut. The lock was so **rusty** it crumbled in his paw.

"Holey cheese, this is more thrilling than a trip to Mouseyworld," Pam whispered.

Slowly, Bridget opened the lid. Everyone **JUMPED** with surprise: Inside the chest was ... **tReasuRe!!!!**

TiME TO GO HOME!

On Monday morning, as they had promised, Bridget, Colette, Nicky, Pamela, Paulina, and Violet were back at **MOUSEFORD ACADEMY**.

The headmaster and **PRofeSSoR RattCLiff** wanted to know everything that had happened. So the Thea Sisters told them the whole tale from the top.

When the **mouselets** finished their story, Professor Rattcliff concluded, "Thanks to the treasure you found, the heir of 𝕸𝖆𝖈𝕹𝖆𝖒𝖔𝖚𝖘𝖊 castle shouldn't have any trouble restoring it."

"No, no trouble at all," Violet confirmed, beaming.

"And because of all the publicity there's been

on TV, soon tourists from all over the world will come **SEE** the castle!" Colette added.

"The restorations will be done following **strict** rules of conservation," Bridget explained. "The castle has been declared a national historic **MONUMENT**!"

Professor Rattcliff nodded with satisfaction. "Well done, **mouselets**! Very well done indeed!"

That was high praise from the professor. The Thea Sisters and Bridget left the headmaster's office feeling **CHEERFUL**.

Bridget in particular was high-spirited. "I've never been able to talk in front of the headmaster without **stammering** before," she confessed to her friends.

"Rock on, **mousefriend**!" Pamela complimented her.

"Our Bridget has **discovered** her inheritance from the great leader Alistair!" Nicky declared, **smiling**.

"She's found the strength and the courage of a true Highlander," Violet added, more seriously.

Colette had a different theory. "No way, mouselets! **Love** has made her stronger and more sure of herself!"

Paulina nodded. "Even if they're apart for a while, Ewan will be waiting for Bridget when she returns to the Isle of Skye!"

Bridget's eyes were **SHINING** at

their words, but she **shook** her snout, **embarrassed**. "What are you squeaking about? You've got it all wrong! It's true that I feel **stronger** after this adventure, but it's because I've found five **precious** friends. I couldn't have done it without you, mouselets!"

They were more than friends. They were sisters!

Thea Sisters

Want to read the next adventure
of the Thea Sisters?
I can't wait to tell you all about it!

THEA STILTON AND THE BLUE SCARAB HUNT

The Thea Sisters have been invited to Egypt to participate in a fabumouse archeological excavation. They are helping to look for the legendary ancient Treasure of the Sun! A precious blue stone scarab may be the key to their search, and they work enthusiastically to uncover the past. But they also discover that thieves are after the hidden treasure. It's up to the Thea Sisters to stop them!

Be sure to check out these exciting Thea Sisters adventures!

THEA STILTON AND THE DRAGON'S CODE

THEA STILTON AND THE MOUNTAIN OF FIRE

THEA STILTON AND THE GHOST OF THE SHIPWRECK

THEA STILTON AND THE SECRET CITY

THEA STILTON AND THE MYSTERY IN PARIS

THEA STILTON AND THE CHERRY BLOSSOM ADVENTURE

THEA STILTON AND THE STAR CASTAWAYS

THEA STILTON: BIG TROUBLE IN THE BIG APPLE

THEA STILTON AND THE ICE TREASURE

Be sure to read these stories, too!

#1 Lost Treasure of the Emerald Eye

#2 The Curse of the Cheese Pyramid

#3 Cat and Mouse in a Haunted House

#4 I'm Too Fond of My Fur!

#5 Four Mice Deep in the Jungle

#6 Paws Off, Cheddarface!

#7 Red Pizzas for a Blue Count

#8 Attack of the Bandit Cats

#9 A Fabumouse Vacation for Geronimo

#10 All Because of a Cup of Coffee

#11 It's Halloween, You 'Fraidy Mouse!

#12 Merry Christmas, Geronimo!

#13 The Phantom of the Subway

#14 The Temple of the Ruby of Fire

#15 The Mona Mousa Code

#16 A Cheese-Colored Camper

#17 Watch Your Whiskers, Stilton!

#18 Shipwreck on the Pirate Islands

#19 My Name Is Stilton, Geronimo Stilton

#20 Surf's Up, Geronimo!

#21 The Wild, Wild West

#22 The Secret of Cacklefur Castle

A Christmas Tale

#23 Valentine's Day Disaster

#24 Field Trip to Niagara Falls

#25 The Search for Sunken Treasure

#26 The Mummy with No Name

#27 The Christmas Toy Factory

#28 Wedding Crasher

#29 Down and Out Down Under

#30 The Mouse Island Marathon

#31 The Mysterious Cheese Thief

Christmas Catastrophe

#32 Valley of the Giant Skeletons

#33 Geronimo and the Gold Medal Mystery

#34 Geronimo Stilton, Secret Agent

#35 A Very Merry Christmas

#36 Geronimo's Valentine

#37 The Race Across America

#38 A Fabumouse School Adventure

#39 Singing Sensation

#40 The Karate Mouse

#41 Mighty Mount Kilimanjaro

#42 The Peculiar Pumpkin Thief

#43 I'm Not a Supermouse!

#44 The Giant Diamond Robbery

#45 Save the White Whale!

#46 The Haunted Castle

#47 Run for the Hills, Geronimo!

#48 The Mystery in Venice

#49 The Way of the Samurai

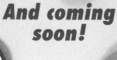

And coming soon!

#50 This Hotel Is Haunted!

Don't miss these very special editions!

THE KINGDOM OF FANTASY

THE QUEST FOR PARADISE:
THE RETURN TO THE KINGDOM OF FANTASY

THE AMAZING VOYAGE:
THE THIRD ADVENTURE IN THE KINGDOM OF FANTASY

Meet
CREEPELLA VON CACKLEFUR

I, *Geronimo Stilton*, have a lot of mouse friends, but none as **spooky** as my friend CREEPELLA VON CACKLEFUR! She is an enchanting and MYSTERIOUS mouse with a pet bat named Bitewing. YIKES! I'm a real 'fraidy mouse, but even I think CREEPELLA and her family are AWFULLY fascinating. I can't wait for you to read all about CREEPELLA in these fa-mouse-ly funny and **spectacularly spooky** tales!

#1 THE THIRTEEN GHOSTS

#2 MEET ME IN HORRORWOOD

#3 GHOST PIRATE TREASURE

THANKS FOR READING,
AND GOOD-BYE UNTIL OUR
NEXT ADVENTURE!

Thea Sisters